7 Sampler Series: Book 7
The Oblique Blade
and 6 more historical tales

Gavin Boyter

7 Sampler Series: Book 7: Historical Tales

First published in 2023 in Great Britain by Sword Pen Press (an imprint of Gugnug Press, Edinburgh).

Copyright © 2023 Gavin Boyter

The moral right of Gavin Boyter to be recognised as the author of this work has been asserted in accordance with the Copyright, Design and Patent Act, 1998.

All rights reserved.

Wheatfield with Crows was first published in Kithe Magazine, Volume 1.

No part of this publication may be reproduced, stored, or transmitted in any form without the express written permission of the publisher, except reasonable excerpts which may be quoted in reviews or commentary.

Cover Design by Gravity Bone

Set in Garamond (body text and footnotes) and Corbel Light (headers) with Calibri page headers.

ISBN: 9798859671588

www.gavinboyter.com

For those who remember.

Contents

About this Book 1
The Oblique Blade 5
Rain, Blood and Whiskey 21
The Besting of Dandy Jack 27
An Arrow's Arc 39
HMS Killjoy 53
Stardust at the Beehive 67
Wheatfield with Crows 75
The 7 Sampler Series 82
About the Author 83

Acknowledgements

Thanks for their continued support, to my parents, sisters, brothers-in-law, nephews and niece. Many thanks are due to all the magazine, website and anthology editors who appreciated my work enough to publish it, or were kind in their rejections. Appreciation must be shown to the staff of the Foyles Café on Charing Cross Road, and Cliff's on Northdown Road in Margate for providing conducive spaces for writing and dreaming. Gratitude, as ever, to my London friends, especially Aradhna, Guy, Sara, Rob H and Indy, to whom I have read some of these stories or received authorly advice. Thanks to my new Margate friends too, for keeping me sane during the transition from the capital to the coast. Lastly, but not leastly, thanks to the London Writer's Café and Ramsgate Writers Unleashed for comradeship and helpful feedback. There will be more…

About this Book

The challenge of writing and selling short stories is that it's very much a niche format. In truth, few people read them, and short stories rarely, if ever, make anyone any money. The heyday of Amazing Stories, Reader's Digest and Harper's paying writers hundreds of pounds for a story has long passed. The golden age of the short story is sadly over.

Although there are fans who collect and enjoy short stories, most successful collections are published by previously bestselling authors trying their hand at the short form. They bring their fanbase with them, in other words.

That said, short story collections do allow writers and readers to explore multiple characters, narratives, locations and genres in one compact package. They offer a taster of the imaginative world of a particular writer (or a host of writers in themed collections) which can be immensely helpful when readers are trying to ascertain who to invest their time in.

Would you embark on a 1000-page novel by a writer whose work you've never sampled? That's a big ask of any reader.

Short story collections offer the security of the finite nature of the format. The short story, even in the literary genre, makes a bold promise: after a few thousand words, each tale will be resolved. Or at least, if not resolved exactly, then certainly *over*. The confusion, the intrigue, the frustration will end (for readers and protagonists!)

I've put together this short, bargain basement sampler, as a way of letting readers dip their toes in the waters of my shortform work, for less than the price of a coffee.

This book is one of seven I will be releasing, which, should you collect the set, will allow you to read 49 of my stories for less than the price of a bottle of absinthe.

This book has a broad 'historical' remit, but within that definition, there are a range of genres and time periods. There are stories set in the Jazz Age, in the medieval era and during the French Revolution. If you enjoy these tales, do turn to the back of the book for a list of the other titles in this series, and my other published works.

If you have fun with these historical stories, you may find much to admire in my collection Running Coyote and Fallen Star, or my crime novel Elena in Exile.

But for now, find a comfy nook, perhaps with a mullioned window, or a yard of ancient flagstones, and let the years roll back…

(Margate, August, 2023)

The Oblique Blade

Tombeau the executioner had grown to loathe his job. At the start of the Revolution, as an apprentice killer, he'd delighted in the spectacle of justice being enacted so finally, and so clinically. His erstwhile master, Marcel Duvalier, who had over a thousand heads to his credit, had been a staunch defender of the oblique blade as a method of dispatch. When a foreign dignitary had dared to suggest that death by guillotine was barbaric, Duvalier had famously retorted, "have you seen the mess you can make of a man's neck with an ill-swung axe?" There had been much laughter, and the visiting ambassador had shrunk back into himself, the very epitome of chagrin.

Duvalier had made a good point. The blade reliably dispatched an average-sized villain in little more than an instant. No more ugly scenes of bodies spasming on the scaffold, or jugulars spraying blood onto the crowd while a felon attempted to crawl to freedom across a slippery river of his own blood. Even Marie

Antoinette had been sent to meet her maker with little more than a whimper and a triumphant roar from the crowd.

But lately, Tombeau, approaching his third year as chief Executioner in Aix-en-Provence, where he'd moved with his young family, was growing disillusioned. All this talk of Liberté, égalité, fraternité, it was beginning to ring hollow. Nothing had much improved in the conditions of the ordinary folk. They were still starving in their squalid millions, even here, in this quiet and picturesque town, surrounded by hills.

Last week he had overseen the executions of forty-eight co-conspirators, who had apparently been communicating with exiled Parisian Girondins. That no evidence of their collusion survived the inspectors' investigation (apparently it burned up in a house fire), was just one more in a series of worrisome events. Was this rooting out of villainy being used to settle personal vendettas, as some of the scurrilous pamphlets in circulation suggested? Was he, Tombeau, a man of integrity, a trained surgeon in a former life, now just another thug working for a different pack of corrupt leaders?

There was something he'd never liked about Robespierre, evident on the few occasions their paths had crossed. The man had conviction, for sure, but he also had a vicious glint in his eye. He took far too much delight in the terror he had created.

Today Tombeau had to execute a sixty-three-year-old printer, of all people, accused of working with the Girondins, printing their anti-revolutionary tracts. The man was elderly, seemed confused by his arrest and baffled by the charges laid against him. Tombeau suspected he was scheduled to be guillotined as a warning against others aiding the forces arrayed against the mission to liberate France from its decadent ruling classes.

"Get him out, won't you? The sun's overhead and the day's wasting!" he found himself shouting as he entered the gaol with two revolutionary soldiers. There would only be one execution today but a crowd of over a thousand had already massed in the Place D'Albertas, to chant their ghoulish curses and gloat.

How he was beginning to hate the world and everyone in it! Perhaps this disillusionment was unsurprising, given his role and the fact that, although concealed by the sombre, black, beaked mask that supposedly granted him anonymity, everyone knew who Tombeau was. Partly because Aix was a small town and whispers scattered as readily as autumn leaves. Mostly because he has six foot four in height and as broad as a wrestler, unmistakable due to the stooped posture he'd developed during an adolescent bout of rickets. Children threw stones at him in the street and ran away, widows muttered under their breath and clutched prayer beads whenever he passed. Even when he was with his wife Madeleine and sons Maxime and Georges, he heard voices mocking him.

Within minutes, the bruised, cowed, and ragged figure of the printer stood before him. He had evidently soiled himself with fear and was shaking like a palsied whippet.

"Go on then!" he shouted at the printer, who twisted his beard anxiously and began to cry, low and soft as if he feared being heard. Tombeau couldn't quite find it in his heart to despise him. The man had a small book clutched in one hand, presumably his bible, as he staggered up the stone corridor towards the bright arch of the doorway onto the street.

As Tombeau and his men marched the printer to his doom, the crowd's roar rose and fell like waves, accompanied by the whinnying of horses and the cries of hawkers, selling cheap wine and whatever mouldy loaves and cheese they could muster. Grain was scarcer than ever before, and bread prices soared weekly.

Abruptly, the soldiers stopped just before the sunlit portal. The printer had fallen to his knees and was clutching at the hem of one of the soldier's jerkins. The officer kicked the miscreant away. The old man picked himself up and beseeched Tombeau instead, unfazed by the implacable raven's beak of his mask.

"Please sir, I am only a humble working man, a good servant of the republic. I print everything – playbills, hymn books, even songs – I allow my clients privacy and control of their treatises, I do not concern myself with their content."

"Get on with you. You know what you've done," Tombeau muttered, pushing the printer towards the light. "I'll drag you there myself if I have to. Face your fate like a man!"

The printer seemed to gather himself together, his attempt at pleading having failed. He almost looked haughty as he replied, huffily, "I am a righteous working man. A good man."

This good man then turned and walked with surprising speed towards the square and his ending. He held out his manacled hands in supplication to the crowd as they either pelted him with rotting cabbages or cried "God be with you!" This latter response to the executions had been building in recent weeks, almost as if some members of the crowd were there to watch martyrs face their ends, not seditious traitors.

The printer climbed the steps, sandwiched between the two soldiers as Tombeau stopped to dip his hands into a small brass bowl of ground chalk, held by a street urchin whose features were incongruously cherubic. Let me get this farce over with, thought Tombeau, and then perhaps today is the day I resign. He rubbed in the chalk, making sure his hands would maintain a steady grip on the rope until the formalities were concluded.

The sunlit square was fiercely bright after the gloom of the gaol, and the smoke from the vendors' stalls blew an ashen pall across the cobbles, carrying with it a strange, sweet smell. Roasted hazelnuts and dried apricots. The smoke rendered everything grainy, unreal, like the way the world looks when you wake in the early morning in winter and your eyes have yet to adjust to the darkness.

While one of the usual magistrates read the charges against the printer and asked him if he had anything to say, Tombeau reached down from the raised stage to snatch a handful of dried apricots and figs from a vendor's stall. The woman behind it nodded her assent, for who would dare to refuse the raven-faced man in charge of the oblique blade?

The apricots were decidedly chewy, as if they had been stored for two long. They began to stick to Tombeau's teeth.

He caught the tail end of the printer's last words, a courtesy the town's magistrate had added as a recent innovation, in an attempt to inject an "opportunity for redemption" into the proceedings. It seldom worked as intended. Most of the victims either wept, remained rigidly silent, prayed, pissed themselves or cursed their accusers violently. More than once Tombeau had had to drop the blade midsentence to spare the womenfolk a choice expletive.

"…and I hope we will weather these dark days and that sanity and kindness will prevail. I am an innocent working man, not a counter-revolutionary! God be with you all."

Whatever else the man had said while Tombeau's thoughts had been drifting, he'd lulled the crowd into an unusually mute state. No more missiles or curses were hurled, and an expectant hush fell as Tombeau helped the printer out of his manacles, gently prised the bible from his hand, and knelt him down upon the stock, placing his exposed nape over the well-smoothed wood, varnished with old blood.

Tombeau lowered the upper stock to meet its kin, padlocking the printer into his final position, supplicant and prone. The executioners adjusted the position of the basket that would receive the victim's head. He ceremoniously ran a finger along the edge of the blade, just a little away from the cutting surface, then raised it to his lips as if injured. Utter theatre, all of it.

The printer was saying something. His executioner stooped to listen. The old man swivelled in the stock to look at Tombeau, whose eyes were the only aspect of his humanity on display.

"Look after my poems. You are a good man."

Tombeau frowned, then looked down at the small book he'd taken from the printer. Not a bible after all, evidently. The old man's face looked almost beatific as he closed his eyes, nodded once, and lowered his head.

Tombeau stood up and made as if to give the mechanism one final inspection. He could see the magistrate frowning at the edge of the stage, wondering what the delay was. The executioner made as if to inspect the rope holding the blade in place, while, with his other hand, he surreptitiously jammed a fig into the groove in the wooden struts which directed the blade to its final destination.

There was an archaic town statute which stated that a condemned man need only suffer three drops of the blade. If the mechanism failed three times, he would be pardoned, since God had evidently seen fit to intervene. There was once a time when nobody would think to argue with God's mercy. The anti-religionists were influential but, in Aix at least, the churches still held their services and Tombeau had frequently seen the magistrate in attendance at the Cathedral.

At the appointed moment, the magistrate swept his hand horizontally in a gesture for both silence and justice. Tombeau unhooked the rope from its cleats and let it go. The blade dropped two feet then jammed in place. A soft murmur rose from the crowd. Quickly, Tombeau stepped up to the scaffold, wound the blade up again before anyone could examine the guillotine. The fig was half-cut through. Tombeau couldn't risk a substitution; all eyes were upon him. He twisted the rope anxiously, then dropped the blade once more. Again, the steel jammed, and this time the crowd gasped and whooped in amazement. Someone shouted, "he has but one more chance!" It wasn't clear whether the onlooker meant Tombeau or his victim, but the magistrate waved his arms furiously for silence and scowled at Tombeau.

"What is wrong with you today, man? Are you entirely incompetent?"

Tombeau bristled but wound the blade up once more. The old man was weeping audibly, mewling like a cat. This was beyond cruel. Tombeau was simply torturing him. He ought to clear the blade's channel and get this over with.

A quick inspection revealed he didn't have to. The fig was gone, but its stalk had somehow wedged itself between the wood and the blade. When he lifted the steel this time, the stalk would drop away, and the blade would be free to perform its duty. Tombeau felt the panic of a conscience in crisis. He had chosen this new path and would not easily be dissuaded. But he couldn't simply refuse to complete the task; there were four keen young apprentices itching to step in. Tombeau could see two of them, Xavier and Laurence, both scarcely eighteen, waiting by the side of the stage. He avoided their eyes.

"Finish him," the magistrate hissed, before adding, piously, "God willing".

Tombeau raised one hand to his mouth as if stifling a cough. As he mimed a final blade check, he spat the half-masticated apricot into his hand and tried to quickly wedge it into the wooden groove. As he did so, he locked eyes with the magistrate.

"What in the name of hell...?" the magistrate crowed, striding over, his polished shoes clacking on the boards. He pushed Tombeau back, leaning under the blade to examine the mechanism. With a look of vicious triumph, the magistrate ran his fingers up the wooden groove, his body off-balance, seeking apricot residue to prove Tombeau's treachery.
It took only a tiny motion of Tombeau's right foot and elbow to trip the magistrate, so that he fell forward across the scaffold. In the same instant, Tombeau let go of the rope.

The magistrate made the terrible, but understandable mistake of twisting to arrest the blade with his hands as it fell. The steel took off four fingers as it sliced down into the magistrate's arm and shoulder. There were screams and the crowd began to surge in all directions. Soldiers ran to prevent townspeople from ascending the steps, while Tombeau quickly lifted the blade from the screaming magistrate, whose arm was sliced open like a side of pork. A bloody chunk of forearm slid down the bald pate of the printer. The condemned man shook as the magistrate writhed across his back, but he remained oddly silent.

Tombeau tied off the blade and, with the aid of one of the soldiers, carried the now unconscious magistrate off the scaffold. While the soldier and others were attending to His Honour, Tombeau lifted the stocks, and yanked the printer back onto his haunches.

"Go. Go now!" he hissed from under the bird mask. The printer seemed lost in an uncomprehending reverie. Perhaps he thought he had died, and this was hell. Tombeau, looking down, realised he was soaked in blood. He heard someone calling his name, angrily. Tombeau knew that tone. He would be next on the scaffold.

"Go on with you! Godspeed!" he shouted into the face of the printer, who seemed to snap out of his trance, as two waiting men pulled him down from the stage. They looked familiar – perhaps they were his sons.

Whoever they were, they threw a blanket over his head and the crowd seemed to open and close like a pair of curtains, concealing the printer, while soldiers attempted to push through the crazed, screaming, weeping, laughing crowd.

Tombeau felt a hand grasp him roughly by the shoulder. A military grip. He ignored it. He wanted to watch the printer vanish out of the square with his sons. He wanted to feel he had done the right thing. He wanted vindication. He wanted to wash his hands, literally and figuratively, of the whole squalid scene.

When the blow came that knocked him unconscious, Tombeau welcomed it, even as his legs folded beneath him and the raven's mask smashed and scattered bark fragments across the blood-soaked boards.

Rain, Blood and Whiskey

Dear Marge

I'm writing this in a quiet spell. The fighting's been intense for the last few months. We haven't advanced since October, due to the weather, and that's frustrating but also brings respite, since they won't send us over the top until the storms break. The lads' morale is low and almost every night we hear some poor chap crying out in his sleep. It sounds like banshees or the souls of the dead echoing through the trenches. Sometimes the sounds float across from the German side too, about a quarter of a mile away. It's almost reassuring, knowing both sides are going crazy out here.

Thanks for the letter and the drinking flask you sent for my birthday. It only took five weeks to get through this time. The other lads are jealous, and I'm amazed – so extravagant! It's the only shiny thing in all this filth and dirt. The whiskey keeps me warm when I'm on night sentry duties so I'm trying to ration it, although I gave some to Charlie Fullbright – we had to pick a bit of shrapnel out of his thigh – the whiskey took his mind right off the pain. They invalided him out and I suspect he'll be in the field hospital by now.

I'm afraid he was the lucky one — a couple of other boys didn't make it that day. We couldn't even retrieve their bodies or give them a decent burial. We had to leave them out in No Man's Land, at least for now. That was the last time we heard the guns — eleven days of rain and silence. I don't know which is worse.

You'd think the silence would come as a blessed relief. When the shells stop landing, blasting mud and stones into our faces, all we hear is rain and the wind howling across the trenches and, closer to home, I hear Wilf forever scribbling in his notebooks.

You writing a novel? I ask him.

Poem, he replies, sharpening his pencil with a penknife. I don't know how he can see anything in the smudgy gloom of the oil lamps.

What's it about? I ask.

Gas, he whispers. For a poet, he's a man of few words. He's a second lieutenant but you'd never know it — he has no airs nor graces about him.

The silence rather throws the waiting into relief and that's what I hate most about it. You know it's going to break and when it does, it's not going to be good. Then there's the rain.
A good hole-free helmet or cap is essential. Otherwise,

when you're on sentry duty, the rain will run down your neck and soak you down to your boots. I've taken to balancing a couple of planks on the metal plate that protects the loophole and then I hide under that. But the rain is clever. It worms its way around everything and then the sappers work hard to channel it away. Thing is, the more we tramp down the dirt, the harder it becomes and the more water it holds when it rains. Sometimes we're practically knee deep in it. The other week the latrine overflowed. The smell was horrifying.

It's about three fluids in wartime – rain, blood, and whiskey. Keeping one out and diluting the second with the third, if you see what I mean. Our Corporal, Wilson, has got the best dugout. He's an engineer back in Blighty and he's built a sort of twin-level bunk, kept off the floor on stilts made from bricks stood up in concrete left over from the last pillbox construction. He let's whoever is on sentry duty sleep in the lower bunk. He's a good sort is Wilson.

I miss you Marge, I miss you so much I can feel it like a wound – like I'm bleeding internally. I don't want you to worry though. We're a tight little unit and we know what we're doing. Even the Frenchies they've sent to join us know a thing or two. They don't wear berets and striped jerseys, either. They know some great songs and they have better cigarettes. I'm learning some French, ma Cherie. Je t'aime et tu me manques.

Gas. I wish I hadn't thought about it. We heard stories of the mustard gas from a Belgian scout called Jacques who ran over from the western trenches. The latest sort is yellowish, stinks, and it burns you out from inside. We're told to soak hankies in ammonia and keep them on our person. They keep promising us gas masks, but we haven't seen any yet. I don't want to tell you what we do when we run out of ammonia – it 'aint nice. We haven't had a mustard gas attack yet but I'm ready when we do. I hope you don't mind that I'm using your hankie, given that it might save my life.

Wilf says he's writing a poem about honour. I can't believe this is his second time round. He won't talk about what happened to him, just says he spent some time "recuperating" near Edinburgh. Sounds lovely but I'm guessing it wasn't. I reckon he's what they call shell-shocked and maybe that's why he scribbles frantically but won't talk much.

If we can push the enemy back to the canals, they say we'll have recaptured the front. Word has come down from on high that we'll soon be going over the top.

I don't want to worry you but there's a chance I won't be coming back. I just need to let you know that I love you dearly and I'll see you again if I can. I hold onto hope as hard as I hold onto my rifle. Not sure what you think of this, but I named my rifle after you. Margery Lee Enfield. And she deserves your name because she keeps me safe.

I have to stop writing this for a bit because the Lance Corporal's calling me.

[unsigned, Private William "Billy" Cadden, Sambre Canal, November 1918]

The Besting of Dandy Jack

Dandy Jack, as he was known throughout Somerset, hadn't started life as a highwayman. Legend had it he'd begun his career as an ordinary farmhand, working the apple harvests. People said he'd been maltreated once too often by his master and had enacted a terrible revenge. The citizens of the village of Ide, where Jack had been born, and to which he secretly returned from time to time, whispered to one another than the lad, when not quite fourteen, had gotten his master drunk on unreasonably strong scrumpy, locked him in the barn and set it alight, then absconded.

The truth was somewhat more mundane. Jack had struck his master for withholding his pay-packet once too often (Jack was frequently late and often insolent), had stolen the payroll and run away. The fire that had occurred the same evening had been entirely incidental and accidental – probably the old soak being careless with an oil lamp.

Conveniently, since burnt fragments of

banknotes were found under the farmer's body, it was assumed that the rest of the cash had burnt up with the barn. Thus, the fire had saved Jack from extensive pursuit by the local beadle, who cared less about apple harvesting farmers than the public purse (into which he regularly dipped a paw).

Still, it didn't hurt to let such awful stories flourish and develop, and after the boy's disappearance from the parish, Jack left it a good decade before he returned to settle down, under the pseudonym of Henry Rackham, gentleman pig farmer, on the selfsame farm he'd once worked as a lad.

  Jack spent most of his year with his grunting, dirty, but entirely trustworthy charges, but in late springtime, while the pigs grew fat on apples from the overgrown orchard from which Jack had once scrumped, he donned his long black cloak, fancy carnival mask and feathered hat and rode out, as Dandy Jack, the highwayman.

Within a couple of years, Jack had pilfered over a hundred pounds from the coaches that rattled their way along the Bath to London Road. The fine terraces in nearby Bath were summer residences of many of the gentlemen of court who wintered in London Town, Henley, or Windsor. They'd often make the two-day journey south to attend a concert, party or wedding, and Jack would lie in wait, choosing his target with caution and cunning.

Jack was no ordinary robber. An autodidact from earliest childhood, and the son of schoolteachers who died from the pox when he was just six years old, he'd learned enough French to woo some of the more loose-tongued (and loosely corseted) Bath ladies. He'd gain their favour and glean intelligence regarding their comings and goings. In his guise as gentleman farmer, Jack-aka-Rackham, whom the gentlewomen considered a charming rogue, would learn which gluttonous aristocrat or scrofulous priest was sallying forth on Saturday morning. He'd sometimes even find out who his coachman might be, and whether he'd have a "man" with him, an armed guard or manservant charged with carrying a pistol or sword for protection.

Jack would avoid the most glitzy and best-defended carriages, preferring instead those victims who attempted to disguise their wealth with unshowy vehicles and early morning departures. Those gentlemen believed their cunning would be their protection. They were sorely wrong in this estimation.

The previous evening, Jack had camped out under a canvas bivouac, concealed within a hawthorn hedge by a bend in the road. This morning, just after dawn, he climbed a stout oak and found a steady perch in its lower branches. Here Jack could see for half a mile in either direction, whilst being quite hidden by foliage. His clubfoot ached as he sat with it curled beneath him. A birth defect, Jack's thickened left sole imparted a louche roll to his walk, which had garnered him the secondary soubriquet of Limpin' Jack.

He held onto a piece of string in one hand, which extended down to a low spar and then, unseen, stretched thirty feet along the hedge to the trap he'd set. When the sound of snorting horses and a plume of animal breath clouded the chill spring air, Jack lay back, tightened the line, and waited. He could hear the rattling of cartwheels and some high-pitched laugher.

Lady Madeleine de Clerc, courtesan to Sir Edwarde Montagu, Earl of Hereford, her voice a bell pealing through the honeyed air. Gentleman farmer Henry Rackham had attempted to woo Maddie a few evenings earlier, during her post-prandial around the circus in Bath. She'd not shared much about her coming weekend other than that she had agreed to accompany a "friend" to town for a wedding. A little more digging from her maidservant revealed that this friend was Sir Edwarde.

Maddie's companion would prove a perfect mark if all went according to plan. By all accounts the man was a terrible coward, a cheat at cards and a bully. The three tendencies often went hand in hand, Jack had discovered.

As the carriage turned the corner, a narrow

two horse gig built for commuting, Jack yanked on the string and pulled the peg out from under the stout log he'd propped up thirty feet away. The log rolled into the roadway, blocking the carriage's point of exit on this narrow lane between tall hedges. Jack levelled his musket and fired a warning blast across the roof, all but blowing its driver's hat off. Jack was a sure shot, however, and knew what he was doing.

As Jack leapt down into the roadway, nonchalantly dropping a fresh ball into the musket, the coachman comically jumped down from his seat and tried to prise open the doors of the carriage. Unsurprisingly, its inhabitants wouldn't let their servant enter, so the driver ran to cover behind the conveyance instead.

"Behold my pretties!" Jack announced, swirling his velvet cloak around his shoulders to reveal his dagger sheath, while leaning the sawn-off musket across the crook of his right arm, "Dandy Jack, at your service. I'm afraid I must now relieve you of your possessions." There was a whispering from within the gig, as the driver ducked back out of sight, muttering some sort of prayer.

"We have nothing but a few pounds, sir, if that will suffice."

The voice was Madeliene's, and she slid the widow shutter aside to reveal her pretty red hair, lace bonnet and a wink she concealed from her paramour. Sir Edwarde sat scowling by her side, arms folded across his chest, refusing to look at Jack.

Madeliene retrieved a small purse from her milk-white bosom and handed it over. She also unclipped her necklace, as Jack's eyes lingering rather too long on the silver locket that decorated her cleavage. She didn't seem at all surprised or alarmed by this turn of events. Jack wondered if his mask, and his affected aristocratic accent wasn't fooling Maddie at all. Did she know who was robbing her?

Jack looked inside the purse. Less than five pounds. Scarcely worth the night he'd spent shivering under a hedgerow.

"I don't believe a fine lord and lady like yourselves would be travelling to nuptials without a present of some sort," Jack said, leaning into the carriage and pointing his musket squarely at the Earl.

By God, the man was ugly. Easily thirty year's Madeleine's senior, Sir Edwarde had a dull grey mole on his chin, from which was protruding two hairs, each at least a quarter inch long. He had more chins than titles and was breathing at a pace that betrayed his true state of mind – Edwarde was frightened.

"We have, no… nothing," Edward stammered. "Bested at cards. Go…going to make a withdrawal in the City. You should have waylaid us on the way back, perhaps?" Edwarde attempted a laugh to accompany his witticism, but it was unconvincing.

"Since you're a gambling man, Eddie," Jack said, "I'll wager I can shoot that ugly wart right off your face. What say you? This purse against whatever's under your lady's skirt?"

Edwarde frowned and leaned stiffly over Madeliene, who had pulled up the hem of her skirt to reveal a glimmer of gold.

"Damn you!" Edwarde muttered, slumping

back down It wasn't clear if he was referring to his paramour's betrayal or to Jack. It didn't matter. Jack lifted a gold bathing set from between Madeliene's ankles and turned it in the light. The basin and jug were beautifully detailed with etched scenes of carousing nymphs and satyrs. Better still, curled within the jug's neck were a few letters, which Jack threw into the dirt, but also twenty crisp pound notes, which he did not.

Jack pocketed his prize and tossed the wedding gifts onto the grassy verge, so that he could keep a steady hand on his musket. It was often at moments like these, when distracted by the prize, that a journeyman thief could come unstuck. Jack knew he had nothing to fear from the inhabitants of the carriage, but what about the coachman? The man peered out from behind the gig, a steely look in his eye. Was he concealing a pistol or knife?

Jack walked towards the driver, gun tilted back over his shoulder, other hand retrieving a single banknote from his inside pocket. He placed a finger to his lips then, out of sight of the Earl and Madeleine, offered a pound to the man. After only a flicker of hesitation, the driver emerged from his hiding place, smiled crookedly, and pocketed the gift.

"Take them swiftly to town and no stopping for beadles," Jack warned, and the driver nodded as he mounted the carriage and took up the reigns. Moments later, the carriage was rattling on down the gravelled lane, the horse whinnying with effort.

Then, as Jack was crouching to pick up his ill-gotten gains, he heard a shriek and the banging of a carriage door.

While the gig raced away around the bend, Madeleine lay sprawled near a muddy puddle, her petticoats bunched up around her knees, leaning on her forearms to avoid her face touching the claggy mud. Jack raced to help her up.

"That's what I get for saving that lobcock from a bullet!" she winced, accepting Jack's hand. "He hit me, the bastard!" Her expression changed. "Do I know you, sir?"

Madeliene's lips formed a thin smile as she brushed at her skirts, trying to remove some of the dust from the road. Jack checked his mask was in place and, flustered, cleared his throat.

"I rather think not. I do wonder why a fine young lady such as yourself would consort with such a fat ugly toad, however."

"Well, that's a whole sorry tale, and no mistake," she said, letting her own dulcet tones slip into a rather more urban mode. It appeared they were both affecting a station to which neither belonged. "Why not take that money you stole from my purse," Maddie suggested, "and buy me my luncheon, in some nearby tavern. Maybe I'll tell all? I take it you've a nag concealed hereabouts?"

Jack's three-year-old stallion, Goose, was tied up behind the hedgerow. Jack took Madeliene's arm and led her along the path, the trinkets and musket uneasily balanced on his other arm. If Maddie moved to grab his gun now, he might not be able to react in time.

She did nothing of the sort, of course. When they reached Goose, Maddie simply placed one dainty foot in the stirrup and vaulted up onto the animal with practiced ease.

"I take it you'll be walking?" she asked imperiously, as Jack stowed his weapon and prizes away in the leather bag that filled the space behind the single saddle.

"I guess I shall," Jack said, with a smile, leading Goose away from the shade of the hedgerow, whilst feeding him a couple of crab-apples.

"And you can lose the party mask, Mr Rackham", Madeline said, adjusting her bonnet. "I'd recognise that limp anywhere."

With that, she kicked the horse into a full gallop and, annoyingly, Goose obeyed his genteel new rider and left Jack in the dust, clutching a half-eaten crab-apple. He laughed, tore off his mask and began to hirple down the London Road after Maddie, wondering if she'd slow down for him, or lead him a merry dance instead.

That was the first, but not the last time Dandy Jack was bested by his quarry.

An Arrow's Arc

King Bjorn was at his wit's end. His son Knud would inherit the kingdom in a little over a year's time, as per the traditions of their land, when Bjorn reached his fiftieth birthday. However, Knud had little more sense than a bloodclot, but was scarcely as useful. He was unruly, hasty, cruel, and lazy. As things stood, he would make a terrible and despotic king.

Knud ordered his classmates beaten when they outstripped him in the schoolroom, and once had a love rival's hands doused in hot tar. The only man he respected was his father. Knud had never known his kindly and wise mother, sadly. Queen Frida had gone to her eternity in childbirth, Knud her only child.

In secrecy and desperation, Bjorn called his councilmen together, swore them to secrecy and relayed his fears. After some hesitancy, since nobody wanted to displease even the mildest Bear King in history, each councilman offered their suggestions. One thought that a spell amongst the raiding parties might instil discipline and bravery in young Knud, now just fourteen summers old. Bjorn shook his head, for he feared for his son's life under such dangerous circumstances. Another advisor counselled that a severe moral tutor might be sought amongst the priesthood. Bjorn scoffed; the lad wouldn't tolerate being told what to do by anyone but himself, let alone a disciple of Odin.

Bjorn was momentarily distracted from his consultation by the realisation that there was another man in the room. Someone was present, who had gone quite unnoticed until now. The king was about to call for the castle guards when he recognised Halfdan, the bowyer, whom he had engaged to create a magnificent longbow for the summer solstice festival. Halfdan was sitting quietly polishing his creation, waiting for the right moment to present the elegant weapon to his King. How the bowyer had sneaked past the guards remained a mystery.

"Er, I might take the boy, as an apprentice," said Halfdan in that oddly diffident manner he had, "if it please my liege."

Two weeks later, at the first cock's crow, a surly and yawning Knud Bjornson presented himself at Halfdan's workshop, flanked by two guards Bjorn had engaged to make sure the boy attended his apprenticeship. Halfdan immediately noted that the boy was gobbling down half a pie and tossed him a wet rag.

"You'll clean those, er, paws before touching anything inside," Halfdan warned. Knud began to protest and made as if to turn tail when the implacable guards sidestepped to bar the doorway.

"Orders of the king,", one guard muttered. With a shrug, Knud turned back to the bowyer.

"Well, let's get on with it," he said, belching and wiping his hands on his tunic in a cursory manner. Halfdan closed his eyes, entertaining brief fantasy of running the lad through with an arrow loosed from his stoutest war bow.

"Lad, you are now an, er, honorary bowyer, an ancient and privileged guild you are ill-equipped to join. You must consider this, er, apprenticeship contractual, and me your absolute ruler. King Bjorn has delegated your, er, care and instruction to me."

What Halfdan was saying was almost blasphemous, but to their credit, the guards did not flinch. Despite his hesitant speech, the absolute certainty in the bowyer's eyes brooked no contradiction. Knud nodded.

"Let's make a damned bow then," he said.

Of course, it wasn't as simple as that. Knud was eager to get straight to grips with a piece of fine, six-year aged yew but Halfdan laughed at the concept.

"First we locate green wood," he stated.
"Then?" the boy asked truculently.
"Then, er, you'll make a dozen terrible bows," Halfdan admitted.

They rode out into the hazel wood behind Halfdan's shop and spent an entire day chasing down a single perfect sapling – one that grew straight, without branches, to seven feet in height, with the circumference of Knud's spindly forearm.

"Why is this taking so long?" the prince moaned towards late afternoon.
"Because you, er, cannot make a fine bow from a crooked, er, shaft," Halfdan replied,

wondering if the boy would miss his rather obvious metaphor. Knud did, of course, since he was busy tormenting a stag beetle with a couple of twigs.

Once they had identified and cut down the green wood sapling, Halfdan spent a week taking the lad through the laborious process of stripping the shaft of its bark, locating, and marking the bow's profile and painstakingly removing layer after layer of wood, with hatchet, drawknife, and rasp. The boy complained endlessly about how tedious the process was. Halfdan cursed under his breath and fought to maintain an even tone.

"It takes time and effort to, er, shape anything worthwhile. There are no shortcuts," he explained, his lesson once more falling on ignorant ears.

Knud left Halfdan's workshop after that first week with hands covered in blisters, aching arms and a determination never to return. As far as the prince was concerned, he told his designated master, he'd just spent a week "making a cruddy fencepost." Looking at Knud's first attempt at a bow shaft, Halfdan was inclined to agree.

"Practice makes perfect," he offered instead. It wouldn't do to send the boy home entirely disconsolate.

Knud spent a good hour that evening attempting to persuade King Bjorn that learning to handcraft a bow was a pointless, thankless, and irrelevant task, but his father remained adamant. The next morning the lad was frogmarched back to Halfdan, who set about demonstrating how to identify the stringline of a bow and how to work around any knots and imperfections he might discover in the wood.

"When you hit an, er, obstacle," Halfdan said, while Knud nursed a skinned knuckle, having slipped with the rasp, "work, er, with it, not against it. Don't fight the wood, let it, er, instruct you. A wise, er, craftsman listens to what the world is telling him."

Knud nodded sullenly, still missing the point. Halfdan sighed. Was this child really the son of King Bjorn, the wisest ruler for centuries?

Three weeks into his apprenticeship,

Halfdan took Knud to a different forest, one in which royal hunting parties habitually roamed, questing for boar and stags. Here there was an ancient Yew copse where only the royal bowyers were allowed to cut saplings. As Halfdan explained this, he led the lad to the bole of an ancient Yew, its trunk twisted and convoluted like knotted rope.

"This tree is, er, over two thousand years' old," he told Knud. Remarkably, the boy's eyebrows lifted – evidence of the first genuine emotion the prince had expressed bar boredom or frustration, since he'd entered Halfdan's charge.

"Older than the kingdom?"

"Considerably," Halfdan said. "And here stood its, er, only child," he added, gesturing to a grey cross-section of hacked-away sapling. "Cut down in its prime."

The boy gulped, involuntarily. "What happened?"

"I cut it," Halfdan said, "The wood is now, er, seasoning. Has been these six years."

"For a longbow?" the boy asked, with something perilously close to enthusiasm.

"Indeed. It takes time to shape a worthy shaft, er, for a prince's bow. It will form your, er, graduation piece."

After this revelation, Knud's attitude changed. He knuckled down, learning to concentrate, discovering within himself a wellspring of effort that neither of them would have believed existed several weeks before. Halfdan saw that it was time to teach Knud the arcane art of tillering.

The boy's fifth greenwood bow was passable enough to endure this process of gradually drawing the bow over a mechanism which measured how many pounds it took to pull back the string, how far it could readily be drawn and, most vitally of all, the precise shape of the curve that resulted as the wood gave under applied pressure.

"A good bow bends evenly, on both sides, describing a, er, perfect arc," Halfdan explained. "It does not warp or shatter."

"So what makes a great bow?" Knud asked, a lump in his throat as he pulled back the rope that drew the bowstring back. There was a creak, and then a crack as he did so, and his bow, drawn impetuously far, split, and exploded from the tiller, a shard of wood embedding itself in Knud's wrist. The boy yelped like a kicked deerhound.

"Patience, Knud," Halfdan replied, reaching for a needle to draw the splinter from the prince's arm. "Your next one will be better."

After eight weeks of apprenticeship, Halfdan greeted Knud one morning with a shaft of yew in one hand, as sturdy as a shepherd's staff.

"You're, er, ready, lad," he said, quietly wondering if he was speaking the truth or just wanting rid of the boy. Haldfan hadn't spent so long in another person's company since he himself was apprenticed, some thirty years prior, and it brought back uncomfortable memories. Halfdan's teacher would punish poor performance by leaving an arrowhead in the fire for ten minutes then pressing it against his apprentice's forearm. The scars were still vivid, hidden by Halfdan's long sleeves, memories of his youthful failings. Halfdan, of course, couldn't adopt such strategies even if he wanted to.

Over the next two weeks, as they approached the summer solstice, the bowyer watched the prince becoming engrossed in his task – fashioning a longbow from yew that might befit a warrior.

"This is seven summers, er, seasoned wood Knud," Halfdan reminded his apprentice, "and it cannot be replaced easily. Treat it kindly." He no longer had to underline his lessons with ham-fisted metaphors. Knud took everything in now; he listened. Halfdan dismissed the two guards and told them not to return. Knud no longer needed that iron reminder of his father's discipline.

Remarkably soon, the perfect parenthesis of a bow began to emerge from the yew, under the timidly tender care of Knud's now calloused paws. The longbow was variegated in colour along its length, the natural division of sapwood and heartwood creating a pleasing blonde and red stripe. Like the hair of the king and the late queen, Halfdan noted, but did not say aloud.

Knud painstakingly crafted a perfectly

balanced bow, moving from axe to drawknife to a blade so fine you might shave garlic with it. He tillered his creation no less than a dozen times, finessing imperfections even Halfdan had trouble seeing.

A new fervour developed in the boy's eyes. A perfectionism that finally revealed that Knud was indeed the Bear King's son. Halfdan had witnessed a similar obsessiveness when the king had commissioned the ceremonial solstice longbow that now adorned the wall of his throne-room. In a few days' time, it would be used to shoot the first arrow of the longest day. Halfdan has never worked so long and hard to please a client; he still had the callouses to prove it.

What eventually emerged, after the tillering, stringing, finessing, dressing, and polishing was complete, was a workmanlike, if imperfect, seven-foot-tall longbow. Knud clutched it proudly, reaching for an arrow from one of Halfdan's quivers.

"Not so fast, boy," Halfdan said, placing a hand on the prince's wrist. "First you must learn the art of the fletcher."

This statement saw the return of the deep sighs that were Knud's trademark. But the boy submitted quicker this time, painstakingly mastering the skill of turning arrow stems, forging arrowheads from molten metal, preparing and painting on the copper, resin, and beeswax coating, then attaching the turkey feather flights with silk. After two weeks' hard work, Knud's working days stretching from eight to ten to thirteen hours, the prince had a quiver full of arrows he had made himself.

Once more, Knud stood at the threshold of Halfdan's workplace, nothing between him and the testing ranges beyond, holding the bow in imitation of a military archer, eager to finally try it.

"I'd better give it a go," Knud said solemnly to his master. "Else how can I complete the final adjustments?"

Halfdan couldn't help but smile. The boy thought he was being cunning. For a split second, the bowyer considered breaking his apprentice's bow over his knee and telling him to start from scratch, but that would be impossibly cruel.

Instead, he simply nodded. Then, as Knud strung an arrow to his longbow for the first time, and the polished wood caught the late afternoon sunlight, Halfdan held up a hand.

"Wait!"

Knud lowered his bow, obediently.

"My prince, please can you, er, tell me what you have, er, learned. In fact, tell your father."

Unnoticed by Knud, King Bjorn had ridden to the edge of the testing field, joined by the same two guards he'd first sent to mind his son.

"Yes, tell me boy," Bjorn asked sternly.

Knud smiled, almost as if humouring his father.

"I've learned that important decisions cannot be taken lightly, that I should listen to those with expertise, that a bow will only bend so far, and that patience is a keen virtue," he replied. "I'm not stupid, father."

With that, Knud pulled back the bowstring, and set loose an arrow, which launched itself skyward with impressive pace. Bjorn couldn't help but laugh aloud. It was the first time he had ever felt proud of his offspring. Perhaps he would let his son fire the first arrow of the solstice sun.

Knud's arrow arced into golden sunlight, following its inevitable trajectory, as all present held their breath, waiting to see where it might finally land.

HMS Killjoy

The HMS Killjoy, out of Peterhead, was the pride of the Scottish whaling industry and Charlie Lauriston had been proud to gain his first official commission as a deckhand in August of 1843. After just fourteen months of sailing north Atlantic waters picking up right whales, sperm whales and even the occasional basking shark, at the age of just seventeen, Charlie received the nod he'd been hoping for. First mate, Mr Buxton, a doughty Englishman from Hull, informed Charlie he was wanted for the southern passage, for a long voyage round the Falklands and on to Antarctica, to hunt the minkes and fabled blues.

"Really?" Charlie said, trying to hide his excitement. He'd been seventeen for four weeks and there were men in The Twa Corbies Inn who might recall his voice breaking. It was very important that he be deemed one of the men, and not just a superannuated cabin boy.

He could scarcely believe his luck, but that's what came of sailing with Captain Adam

Robertson, one of Peterhead's most impetuous and successful whaling captains. Robertson had taken 57 whales in 1842 alone, and the evidence was there on his vessel for all to see – a gold leaf fish for each kill, painted on the prow, just above Killjoy's name scroll.

"Really, son. Now you'd better down that beer and go pack your trunk – we're leaving tomorrow morning at six," said Buxton, who'd always been something of an uncle to Charlie. Charlie knew when he was onto a good thing and did as he was told.

The following morning, as a tobacco-hued first light glanced through the lace curtains of his tiny attic room, Charlie yawned, stretched, and dragged himself awake. The day was chilly – late-August but already there was a biting hint of winter in the haar. Forty minutes later, with a belly full of porridge and coffee, Charlie dragged his wheeled trunk down onto the dock and over the cobbles, sending seagulls flying.

There she sat, bobbing in the drydock, newly de-barnacled, caulked, and ready to go – HMS Killjoy, a fine two masted schooner, with a broad rendering deck and two giant steel trypots waiting for the precious blubber they'd score if Antarctica proved lucrative.

"All aboard boys!" the first mate shouted, and the assembled crew jostled and laughed their way up the gangplank to the lower deck. Some of the men took their leave of wives and sweethearts, their voices gruff as they concealed their emotions. Faces set as solid as the granite of Peterhead dock, the men waved to their families as the deckhands cast off.

Charlie had no sweetheart to say farewell to and for this he was both grateful and ashamed. He would blush and redden whenever he tried to talk to the town's girls, who always seemed to want to tease and baby him. That's all you got when you were seventeen and a virgin, with scarcely a chin whisker in sight and standing just five foot four in your sea boots.

As they rounded the harbour, it felt good to feel the roll and swell of the sea beneath his feet again, as Charlie set to work on his appointed task of washing seagull droppings from the mizzen mast. He didn't mind how lowly his chores were, it all contributed to the success of the voyage. We're all in it together, he thought, a fact demonstrated when they hit their first storm one week out and spent four hours tightening and loosening the capstan with every man's muscles straining at the rotating mechanism, keeping the sails taut, maintaining a true navigation line.

Seamanship was teamwork at its most egalitarian. Charlie pulled alongside Buxton and the black cabin boy Omar – there was no division between the men in a crisis, because division meant death when your enemy was a force 10 gale, and you were sailing eighty miles offshore.

The passage south to the Falkland Isles took almost two months, with brief stops at the Azores, Cape Verde, and Tristan de Cunha. In the latter, at the town named Edinburgh by its Scottish founders, Charlie finally popped his cherry, with a young scullery maid, much to the ribald amusement of his fellow seamen. Before he left Maria, who had a pretty, oval face with freckles randomly scattered across her brow like Caribbean islets, Charlie gifted her a locket his mother had left him, containing a forelock, as per Maria's impassioned request. He vowed to see her again, although he was almost certain this would – and could - never happen.

Two weeks later, the HMS Killjoy made her final stop before the icy southern seas, porting at the much-disputed Malvinas, which were enjoying a brief hiatus of peace under British rule. Charlie had grown a straggly beard for the first time and had earned the nickname Shakespeare, because of the many letters he wrote for Maria, but never sent. Finally, at the Post Office at Port Stanley, he was able to post the bundle, whose size raised the postmaster's eyebrow, the expense costing Charlie almost a week's wages.

The voyage so far had been mediocre in terms of the fish they'd landed. Two medium minkes, one smallish right, a couple of sperm whales and an elderly humpback. Charlie hadn't lost his nausea at the smell of rendered blubber, but he'd learned to dab a couple of drops of whiskey onto his moustache to mask the stench. Less bloodthirsty than his fellow whalers, Charlie preferred to tend to the ropes and pulleys, clean the instruments and leave the flaying and rendering to those with a stronger stomach.

There was also something undeniably heart-troubling about the keening sound of the massive mammals as they traversed the oceans at night. Once, having caught a young sperm whale, the sounds of its mother (presumably) bemoaning the loss of her child had continued for hours, and Charlie had wrapped a pillow around his head and stuffed pieces of wax into his ears to block out the terrible sounds of torment. The irony of that wax having emanated from a sperm whale's oil did not escape him.

They left the Falklands after four days of rest and recuperation, which for many of the men meant drunken philandering and profligate gluttony. Charlie abstained from most of it, thinking of Marie, his departed mother and father and the terrible tales that some of the older seadogs had spun about the Southern Ocean and the long white bergs that crashed and drifted, a peril to any vessel, and to a captain of any proficiency.

"Three ships sunk without a trace in the last year, they tells me," grumbled harpoonist and skilled spoon player Willie McTavish. "Why them fish want to swim here is beyond me."

Charlie had a theory. The whales, he imagined, were like southerners who loved visiting the Highlands for the scenery. Except these Antarctic ranges were inverted, upside down kingdoms of ice and barren rock, concealed from view beneath the waves. The whales probably knew how dangerous these waters were for the ships that preyed upon them, too, and perhaps assumed they'd evade capture there. Frequently, they were right. The ratio of sightings to kills was low here and plagued by storms, high seas, hidden bergs, and seemingly endless nights, the South Atlantic was no place for chancing misadventure.

Yet, on October 14th, 1843, in the midst of a terrible storm, a misadventure was exactly what befell Charlie Lauriston. The Killjoy had been pursuing a rare treasure – an Antarctic blue – fully sixty feet long – far too big to fit on deck in one piece of they ever landed her, so she'd have to be sliced up in the ocean first. Nevertheless, this fish would be worth the trip to the frozen south alone. Charlie calculated she must have 450 gallons of spermaceti in her immense head, and perhaps a hundred barrels of oil in her blubber too.

"A floating fortune", Captain Robertson had described her, ordering all men to their positions, and drawing deep on his skrimshander meerschaum. McTavish had already fired three harpoons at the fish, although only one had hit its target. It seemed to trouble the blue no more than a splinter would a cabin boy. Moments later, the storm hit.

Scowling out of the early evening dark came an ash-grey stormfront, with pelting rain and unpredictable blasts of rain. There was thunder and lightning too, and Buxton started telling stories about ships supposedly hit by lightning and blasted into flame, until McTavish told him to "haud his wheest" because he was trying to concentrate on loading another harpoon.

They were getting ever closer to the looming white edge of an ice-pack. If the whale swum under it, they'd lose her. But if they sailed too close, they might never get out of the crescent bay of ice and rock. The men, muffled and wrapped in layer after layer of fur and oilskin had to signal mutely to one another, since the storm wouldn't permit their voices to carry further than each man might spit.

After almost an hour's pursuit, Buxton suggested to his Captain that they might draw back, and leave the fish to perish from what was surely a lethal shot. Captain Robertson knew exactly what Buxton was doing. He was intimating that Robertson had taken leave of his senses. Roberston coolly exhaled a cloud of reeking pipe smoke and ordered his first mate to persist with the pursuit.

So it was that, as twilight merged into dusk, the HMS Killjoy grazed a largely submerged fragment of ice, some fifty feet long and just as deep. The sound of the collision made a terrible grinding racket. The men fought with the tiller and the sails as the ship listed, and a sail whipped free and slapped Charlie

Lauriston suddenly overboard. Hidden by the storm and by the very sail that had assaulted him, the boy plunged unseen into the icy water, and the Killjoy sailed on.

Charlie knew he'd sink and drown if he didn't shed his outer layers. He also knew he'd be dead within minutes if he succumbed to the terrifying cold. As he watched the receding schooner slide off the berg and bank away from danger, leaving him to his fate, Charlie wriggled free from the heavy fleece jerkin and oilskin and bellowed himself hoarse. He knew it was futile, although the attempt felt mandatory. Even if Charlie's shipmates could hear his cries, they'd never be able to locate him. The thought was moot, in any case. Men overboard were seldom deemed valuable enough to turn back for. Not lowly deckhands, at least.

Charlie struck out for the berg, thinking that if he could at least climb out of the raging, icy waters he might last long enough for a lifeboat to find him, had one been dropped. At the very least, he might gain sufficient minutes to say a final prayer, think about Maria, and cross the threshold to the next life in some sort of peace.

Moving gave him purpose, so Charlie kicked off his shoes and swum through waves which did, at least, seem to be smaller here, in the lee of the iceberg. He clutched at the ice but couldn't get a single handhold on the pitted, vertical surface. Charlie was worried that the currents might drag him under, as his fingers and arms inevitably weakened. A terrible numbness was engulfing him, spreading from the outer extremities inward. If only he could find an incline gentle enough to drag himself…

Then Charlie heard it. The booming tones of whalesong. Somewhere beneath or beyond him the cetaceans slid – it was now too dark to locate them or see anything with much clarity. But he could hear their song. Charlie tried to sing back at the invisible behemoths. Perhaps, delirious from the icy numbness in his limbs, Charlie thought that by communicating with the animals, they might not rise up to devour or drown him. He would deserve nothing less if they did seek revenge, having contributed to the demise of dozens of their kin.

Something else happened, something inexplicable. A whale breached, just off to one side – the geyser of spray drifting close enough to fall upon Charlie's upturned face, the blast of air and water loud enough to cut through the booming storm. An arc of whalesong called to something deep in Charlie's gut. Without knowing why, he pushed off from the berg and swam out towards that sound.

Charlie didn't find the whale, which must have descended as abruptly as it rose, but, in his attempts to follow its song, he swam unknowingly towards a rocky ridge protruding from the Antarctic shelf. At first, he mistook the triangular shape for the beast he was following, for its mighty tail emerging from the ocean. Instead, the shadow was a spur of rock, and Charlie's feet grazed its edge as he, gratefully but with agonized effort, dragged himself onto the sodden face of the ancient granite.

Charlie's life was inevitably ebbing away as he lay on his back, gazing up at stars which peeped between banks of dissolving cloud.

The storm had broken. The keening of the unseen whale, perhaps even the one they had been pursuing, diminished, and vanished, leaving Charlie's life to dwindle just as certainly. Like the daylight glimmering into darkness as a drowning man sank through murky fathoms, Charlie's thoughts darkened. He felt nothing physical now, no pain at all as saltwater lashed over him, and wind chilled the sail-whipped scar on his left cheek.

And then, another long, distant call. Not a whale this time – a voice.

"Chaaaarliiieeee!"

With much effort, Charlie turned his head, saw a rowboat bobbing on the waves, a lantern at its prow. He closed his eyes, tried and failed to raise a hand, too exhausted to respond, too far gone to feel anything as sharp as relief, simply content to let fate do whatever it must with him.

Stardust at the Beehive

It was ten thirty on a Saturday night and the joint was jumping. The joint in question was the Beehive Club, a 133rd street basement speakeasy 200 yards from the Cotton Club and the Savoy. Although integrated like all the best places, it lacked some of the glamour of those more celebrated venues. The Beehive's clientele was a little shadier, but it was a cooler and more intimate dive. Owner and host was mob boss Slim Hernandez. Nobody really knew where Slim was from – some said Cuba, others Brazil, but he had cornered the local prostitution and protection rackets. The Beehive was his pet project: a bid for legitimacy, a money-spinning melting pot and a hothouse for the coolest swing and big band music around.

At a booth near the stage sat two men and one woman. The men were black, the woman mixed race, but on the pale side. She was a young journalist called Cindy Bruford, who mingled in circles as varied as meat-packing mobsters and midtown grandees. A jazz fanatic, she was keen to catch ex-pianist turned cornet player Billy Fleming's comeback. The older man was sports talent scout Lennie Hampton, the younger star baseball player Fred "Lefty" Capshaw, just signed to the Dodgers, whom Cindy was profiling. Fred had brought Lennie to his frequent hangout as a thank-you. Cindy was a happy tag-along.

The band were playing a single set, as support for The Nighthawks Big Band, since Fleming was making his bandleading debut and they had only begun rehearsals a couple of weeks' prior. Slim Hernandez himself jumped onstage to introduce them – a rare honour.

"Ladies and gentlemen, do we have a treat for you tonight. A brand-new five-piece with a familiar face at the helm, our old-friend Billy "Knuckles" Fleming."

Cindy, eagle-eyed as ever, saw Fred wince at Slim's sardonic use of the nickname "knuckles". She sensed a story and leaned over to get it. Fred looked around before replying. Nobody was paying them the slightest attention - all eyes were on the band as Slim introduced each member.

"It's one hell of a story", Fred began. "Billy was a great accompanist for small groups and signers, including none other than Maeve Sharp, before she had her hits, when she was Slim's main squeeze. Only Billy had his eye on her too and had the bright idea of spiriting her away to Kansas City."

Cindy got her pad out under the table. She'd learned the useful skill of scribbling shorthand notes out of sight. Lennie, a taciturn soul, leaned in too, as eager for the gossip as anyone.

"Towards the end of the night, Billy overplays his hand, blows Maeve a kiss onstage. It's just showbiz schtick but Slim sees it different, storms over and slams the piano lid down. Shatters both of Billy's paws. He only regained use of one of them completely."

Cindy winced but Lennie laughed, as if hearing an urban legend. She'd canvas his opinion later.

The first number had begun, drummer, pianist and bassist working the intro up before sax-player Willie Jackson stated the melody. Take the A-Train, played at lightning speed, as if it might derail at any second. Dancers were already crowding the floor.

Cindy was aware of something shimmering nearby, sequins reflecting the light. She turned and there was a curvaceous young black woman, who looked like she'd been poured into her golden tasselled dress, slashed up to the thigh on one side. The newcomer was sashaying to the music. Cindy overheard Lennie whispering to Fred:

"That who I think it is?"

Fred nodded and Cindy twigged. Maeve Sharp, transfixed by her erstwhile accompanist's grand return.

Then came a piercing, keening note, which floated over the dancers like a flight of migrating birds. All heads turned to the stage, where Billy held the cornet in his one good hand, other thrust deep into his jacket pocket. Billy held that first note as long as he could before falling back into step alongside Jackson. Together they rattled through the verse before Billy took his first solo, a cascade of barely-controlled notes in an excitingly raw tone that reminded Cindy of Bix Beiderbecke. Clearly,

Billy was a man for whom music was a vital force that had to come out. If not with ten fingers on a keyboard, then with three on a horn.

The first song ended, dancers and drinkers alike exploding into applause. Slim beamed from the side of the stage, holding his trademark highball. Cindy, whose journalistic eye was always straying away from centre stage, saw Slim's smile change to a scowl. He had spotted Maeve, who, it had to be said, was hard to miss. The singer shimmied between tables towards the dancefloor. Billy saw her and beckoned to his pianist, who unhitched his vocal mike and tossed it over. Billy tapped it, ensuring he could be heard.

"Folks, we got an extra special surprise for our next number. None other than Miss Maeve Sharp!"

Slim's eyes threw daggers at the man he'd sadistically mauled, looking like he might bite off the remaining hand. Billy ignored him. Maeve took the mike and, lifting her sequins with one hand, gingerly ascended to the stage. "Thanks everyone," she said, lowering her head with false modesty, before announcing the song with a single word: "Stardust".

A hush fell over the crowd. Fred turned to whisper to Cindy.

"That's what they were playing when Slim… you know."

Hoagy Carmichael's classic oozed magnificently into the room, with Billy and Willie trading licks on the snaky melody before Maeve began to sing:

Sometimes I wonder how I spend the lonely night

Dreaming of a song.

Billy raised his horn and the rhythm section hushed, allowing a duet of horn and human voice to burnish the song to a bright sheen. Billy gazed lovingly at the singer; Maeve flicked little glances at the cornetist. Nobody in that room, least of all Slim, was in any doubt that this was a declaration of love – real love, not the sugary, sentimental kind that Tin Pan Alley traded in.

For the final chorus, the whole band took up the melody and wringed it of every emotional droplet. Once again, the crowd erupted. Slim strode along the front of the stage while Maeve coiled the mike cable and made to return it to the pianist. Slim grabbed her arm, aggressively. Abruptly Billy took his gnarled, ruined right hand from his jacket. This time, the metal that flashed between his knuckles wasn't a horn. There was a bang, a flash of light and Slim clutched his chest, falling back from the stage, dancers parting as he hit the deck. Maeve and Billy, hand in hand, exited stage left while chaos descended.

Cindy was later interviewed by the police. She told them that Billy had fired in self-defence. Slim would have killed the cornet player if he'd not shot first. Of that she was sure. It didn't matter – there was more at stake than crime and culpability.

There was music and love and revenge. And, it went without saying, there was Cindy's first front page.

Wheatfield with Crows

Yesterday I burned three paintings in the yard at the Auberge. The acrid smell as the oil paint blackened and curled away from the browning canvas satisfied me deeply. It gave me as much pleasure as cooking sausages over a campfire had when I was a boy.

Dr Gachet cycled by and threw his bicycle down, rushing up the lane to stop me. The pain in his eyes was almost comical.

"Vincent! What are you doing?" he said, coughing in a curl of blue smoke.
I held him from the flames with an outstretched hand, as I dropped the last work into the brazier. He tried to grab the edge of a frame, just as it's varnish caught the flames. The old fool would set fire to his beard if he weren't careful.

"I'm removing ugliness from the world," I explained. I couldn't help feeling a sliver of sadistic pleasure as my old friend struggled to comprehend what he considered an atrocity. I don't know where he gets his boundless sentimentality – those works were inferior, inauthentic, wrong. I tried to explain but he just kept bleating – "at least keep the frames and paint over the canvases!" It cheered me up – watching him blow on his burnt fingertips and do a little dance of fury in the garden.

"Old friend," I told him. "You mustn't worry so. It will damage your health."

We both laughed, since we are already ruined and I am convinced the good doctor will perish first, despite his homeopathic remedies, which I am sure are simply water blessed by naïve optimism.

It's a great pity the farmer and his boys will come with their scythes soon. In a matter of days, the wheatfields will be razed to a stubble shorter than my own. I paint with diagonal dabs and slashes that are filled with urgency. Midsummer will be upon us, then just as quickly autumn with its scatterings, before winter throws a shroud over the Val d'Oise. Each season races by with a terrifying acceleration. I paint like a man frenzied by the scythes coming up behind him. In just three

years I will be forty! What have I achieved?
Nothing! Everything! I oscillate between
these conclusions.

I long for Theo and Johanna's next visit.
Someone sane should remind me that what I
do each day is worth doing. They departed,
last week, my infinitely patient brother, his
wife and their little boy. They've named him
Vincent. I wept when they told me.

The field is like a stretched canvas, like a
pair of open palms. A steady wind slants the
sheaves to the right, causes the crows to wheel
drunkenly on its turbulence. I try to capture
this motion against a darkening azure sky. I'm
tempted to look at my pocket-watch – a
present from Dr Gachet. I refuse to do it.
What need have I of clocks? I can tell by the
shadows and the deepening blue that I have an
hour and a half of sensible daylight. It is
enough. I pull my coat tight around my neck
and force the cap down over my ears. I really
ought to obtain a scarf.

Honey, cocoa and asparagus. The colours of
the field make me momentarily hungry, but the
thought passes with a shot of absinthe from

the flask in my inside pocket. It's astringent bite never fail to warm me. Perhaps I will eat in the tavern on my way home, if the landlady will extend my credit. The money Theo left me has all but flown.

I fill a flat, medium-sized brush will a daub of burnt umber, to delineate the pathway cutting between the fields and zig-zagging out of sight over the hill. It is rutted by the wheels of carts and the hooves of horses, red-brown dirt alternating with stripes of green grass where the wheels cannot reach. I've haven't yet walked that path; I don't know where it leads.

I'm glad I chose this wide canvas and came out today, instead of painting in the Auberge. The mistress doesn't like it when I splatter her floorboards. But its good that I am not cooped up in the Yellow House with lesser painters sneering at my furniture and complaining of cockroaches.

The sun is behind me and I can feel its dying warmth on my neck. I'm glad I don't have to squint. Looking into the sun all day gives me headaches and fills me with fury and frustration.

It's time to do justice to the clouds. They are usually magnificent in early July but today there are just two blobs of blue-white cumulous, rolled like napkins on a restaurant table. Once I have layered them in, to my satisfaction, I'll concentrate on the crows. This painting is really about them, as they wheel and dance, daring one another to dive for worms or nibble at fallen seeds. They resemble the blades of scythes. I dash off several dozen, exaggerating their number, because I want them to merge into the sky. In fact, I'll darken the sky at its fringes, and they can emerge from that unfathomable space above. A murder. That's what the English say, and they know what they are talking about.

I don't feel melancholy today. I rarely do when I'm working. There's just too much to think about when I fill up my mind with colours and textures and shapes. Damnable art critics say my work lacks depth and form and precision, as if truth could be attained by making art like you might take a Daguerreotype, freezing reality onto a plate!

As if there's any truth in the bourgeois depiction of lords and ladies and prancing horses and spoilt ruddy-cheeked children! Give me a weathered farmer, crooked as a hawthorn, tilling his field, or a red-nosed postman drinking away his wages. That's my kind of truth.

But worse than ignorance is the greatest sin of all – pity. I see it in Theo's eyes constantly. And sometimes in the eyes of Dr Gachet, although fleetingly these days because I mostly just frustrate him. I see it in some of the kinder townspeople, wet-eyed and slack-jawed in incomprehension. Why must he stand out in the cold for hours, why must he live on bread, cheese, wine and stolen apples?

Because I must. That's the only answer I'll give them and if it makes no sense then damn them all! There is always the revolver, and the wine. There is always the lovely light just before sunset, the wheatfield before the scythes come, the cackling of crows and the rich red earth under my boots.

The 7 Sampler Series

1: Allies in the Deep & 6 more Horror Stories
2: A Clearing & 6 more Spooky Tales
3: Singularity & 6 more Sci-Fi Stories
4: Merry go Round & 6 more Romantic Tales
5: Lunacy & 6 more Comic Tales
6: Cold Water Shock & 6 more Sad Stories
7: The Oblique Blade & 6 more Historical Tales

About the Author

Gavin Boyter is a Scottish writer now living in Margate, Kent. Having previously worked in advertising and healthcare, he is now concentrating on creative writing and freelance copywriting. In 2018, he ran from Paris to Istanbul, as described in his 2020 book *Running the Orient*. Boyter is also a screenwriter with two optioned projects in development, including the psychological thrillers *Nitrate* (co-written with Guy Ducker) and *20 Questions*.

A documentary film version of Boyter's first running book, *Downhill From Here*, is in the works. In 2021 he released his first collection of short stories, *Running Coyote and Fallen Star* and in 2023 published the crime novel *Elena in Exile*.

Boyter loves running long distances, wild swimming, and will almost certainly never learn to play the guitar properly.

Other Books by Gavin Boyter:

Non-Fiction

Downhill From Here
Running the Orient
Run for the Hell of It

Fiction

Running Coyote and Fallen Star
Elena in Exile

www.gavinboyter.com

GAVIN BOYTER

ALLIES IN THE DEEP

AND 6 MORE HORROR STORIES

"A rare writer who can make a situation far away seem real and relatable"
Lisa C. Taylor, WORDPEACE Fiction Editor

7 SAMPLER SERIES: BOOK 1

GAVIN BOYTER

A CLEARING

AND 6 MORE SPOOKY TALES

"A rare writer who can make a situation far away seem real and relatable"
Lisa C. Taylor, WORDPEACE Fiction Editor

7 SAMPLER SERIES: BOOK 2

GAVIN
BOYTER
SINGULARITY
AND 6 MORE
SCI-FI STORIES
"A rare writer who can make a situation far away seem real and relatable"
Lisa C. Taylor, WORDPEACE Fiction Editor
7 SAMPLER SERIES: BOOK 3

GAVIN BOYTER

MERRY GO ROUND

AND 6 MORE ROMANTIC TALES

"A rare writer who can make a situation far away seem real and relatable"
Lisa C. Taylor, WORDPEACE Fiction Editor

7 SAMPLER SERIES: BOOK 4

GAVIN BOYTER

LUNACY
AND 6 MORE COMIC TALES

"A rare writer who can make a situation far away seem real and relatable"
Lisa C. Taylor, WORDPEACE Fiction Editor

7 SAMPLER SERIES: BOOK 5

GAVIN BOYTER
COLD WATER SHOCK
AND 6 MORE SAD STORIES

"A rare writer who can make a situation far away seem real and relatable"
Lisa C. Taylor, WORDPEACE Fiction Editor

7 SAMPLER SERIES: BOOK 6

Printed in Great Britain
by Amazon